# THE INFLATABLES in DO-NUT PANIC!

# DIVE INTO THE DEEP END
## with more inflatable adventures!

#1 *The Inflatables in Bad Air Day*

#2 *The Inflatables in Mission Un-Poppable*

#3 *The Inflatables in Do-Nut Panic!*

# THE INFLATABLES

### in DO-NUT PANIC!

By Beth Garrod & Jess Hitchman
Illustrated by Chris Danger

Scholastic Inc.

To Pam, Rosanna, Sarah, Becky, James, and Tina,
the best human inflata-buds there could be −BG

For my Dad, maybe the early morning swimming
lessons weren't wasted after all :) −JH

To McCailin Wunder, Sarah Armstrong, Kyle Miller,
Jenny Sullivan, and Shannon "the Cannon" Schuman,
champions of the human race. −CD

ISBN 978-1-338-74901-4

10 9 8 7 6 5 4 3 2 1                    22 23 24 25 26

Printed in the U.S.A.          37

First printing, 2022

Book design by Stephanie Yang and Kay Petronio

# Chapter One

## Sweet Dreams Are Made of Cheese

It was just a normal day at the Have a Pizza Pizza park.

Until . . .

3

SLIP-N-SLICE

-MENU-

CHILI CHEESE
DEEP PAN
PERFECTION

HANGRY HAM
HAWAIIAN HERO

AWESOME
ANCHOVY

**PIPPARONI**

**FUNNY, SMART, CUTE,
THE BEST (AKA DONUT'S
ULTIMATE INFLATA-CRUSH).**

Donut always tried to look his best when going to get pizza.
Perhaps because pizza is the best snack in the world . . .

PUMP
PUMP

. . . or perhaps because a certain inflatable
slice lived at his favorite pizza stand.

But when Donut arrived, something stopped him in his tracks . . . and it wasn't a new topping combo.

Pipparoni! What happened?!

SLIP-N-SLICE

KEEP OUT
KEEP OUT
KEEP OUT
KEEP OUT

—MENU—

CHILI CHEESE
DEEP PAN
PERFECTION

HANGRY HAM
HAWAIIAN HERO

AWESOME
ANCHOVY

**BROKEN HEART**

7

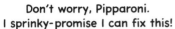

Don't worry, Pipparoni.
I sprinky-promise I can fix this!

But how? The place is empty. A pizza
stand needs customers to survive.
And you're the only fun-guy here.

I'll get more customers than you could
EVER imagine! You can count on me,
Pipparoni. I'm gonna put the *O* in *hero*!

But had Donut bitten off more than he
could chew! (Which was actually quite a lot.)

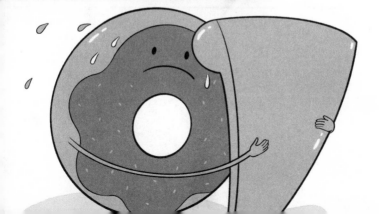

9

# Chapter Two

# Take a Pizza My Heart

What's wrong, Donut-dude? Did they run out of anchovies again?

Even worse. A pizza my heart is broken. Slip 'N' Slice is closing! And Pipparoni is going to be deflated! TONIGHT!

Quick! Emergency snack time.

EMERGENCY SNACKS
POOL EQUIPMENT

Uh-oh!

Okay. *Emergency* emergency snack time!

EMERGENCY SNACKS
POOL EQUIPMENT

IN CASE OF SNACK EMERGENCY
BREAK GLASS

PUDDING! Lynn, you're a genius!

SMOOCH!

A little sugar is the ONLY thing that could make a pizza stand better!

SLIP-N-SLICE

But which dessert is the best one in the whole chewniverse?

Something guaranteed to bring EVERYONE to the stand?

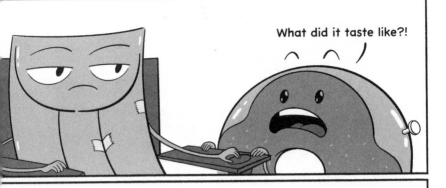

What did it taste like?!

Rainbows, laughter, peace and quiet.

People came from around the world to get their hands on one.

Until one day, only a single cookie was left. And the recipe could not be found. So to keep it from disappearing forever, the last cookie was taken to a top-secret location. And sealed away in a special cookie jar.

How can we find this cookie?

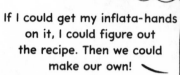
If I could get my inflata-hands on it, I could figure out the recipe. Then we could make our own!

There's only one problem. The map to find the cookie has been hidden away for years.

Noooooooooo!

In my underwear drawer.

Yeeeeaaaaahh!

And ick.

But there's only one problem.

The journey is so dangerous, no float has ever attempted it—and come back unpopped.

Just because it hasn't been done before doesn't mean it can't be done . . .

17

18

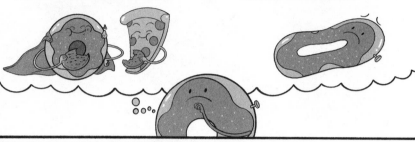

19

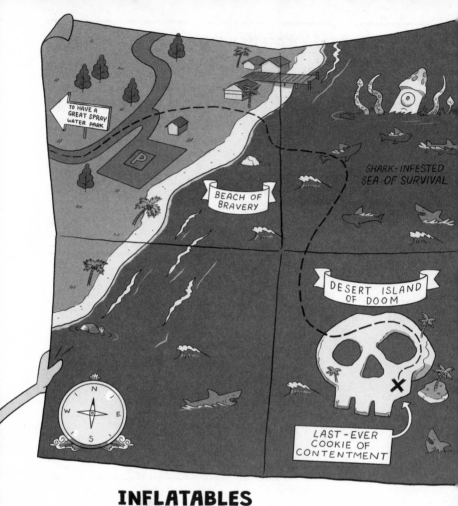

**INFLATABLES ASSEMBLE!**

We've got treasure to find!

# Chapter Three

# Air Revoir, Water Park

This is going to be difficult and dangerous. Everyone pack light—take only what you need to survive.

All we need to do is prop ourselves up against the coach, blend in with the luggage, and they'll load us on board.

Trust me. It's how I managed to tour the world with Air-osmith back in '75.

But what if we get caught?

Don't worry, dough-face. I've got friends in high places. And by high places, I mean the mighty throne at the front of this bus.

Now let's go!

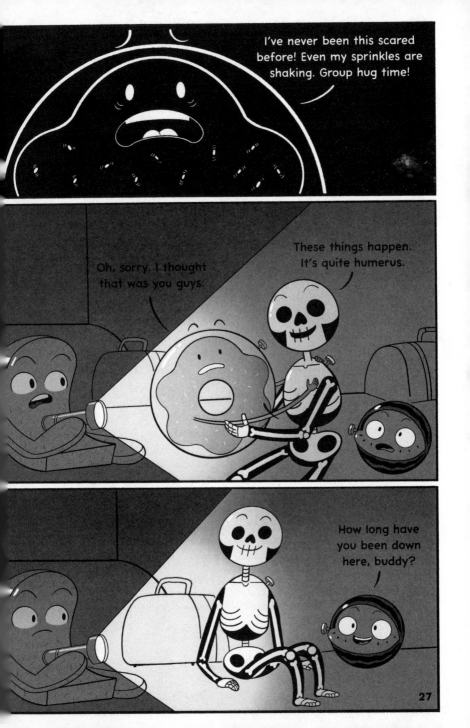

27

Since the great Halloween Cheese-on-Cocktail-Stick Disaster.

Dun dun duuuuuuuun! *SINISTER SOUND EFFECT.*

• RE

Since then, no inflatable has ever made it back from the beach unpopped.

*UNEXPECTED PLOT TWIST.*

GULP.

• RE

And we're SURE there's no other way to get the cookie?

Too late now! We're on the move! Beach of Bravery, here we come!

*TENSION MUSIC.*

• RE

For the first time since they'd met, the Inflatables had left the water park.

HAVE A GREAT SPRAY!

HAVE A GREAT SPRAY BEACH SHUTTLE

WILL THE GANG EVER MAKE IT BACK?! *CLIFFHANGER!*

## Chapter Four

# Beach Air, Don't Care

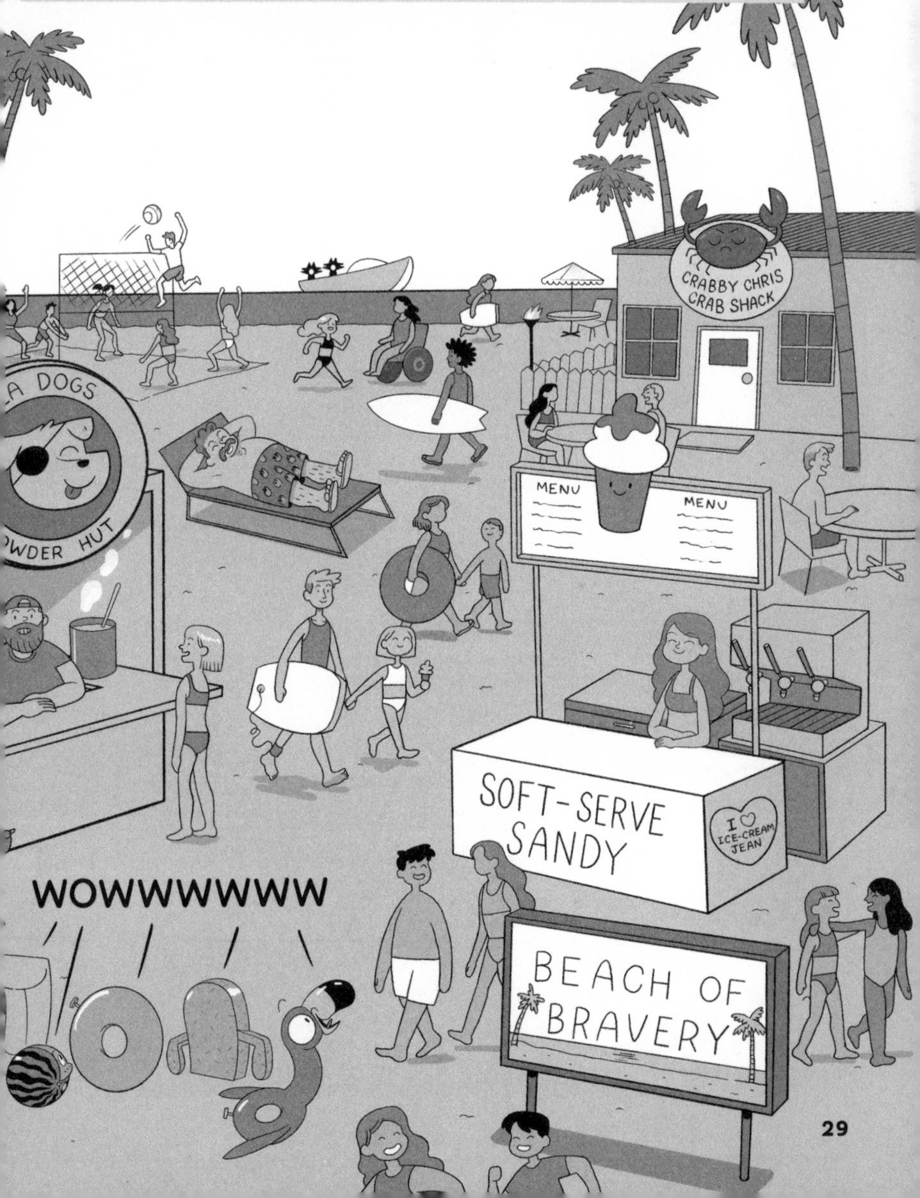

35

39

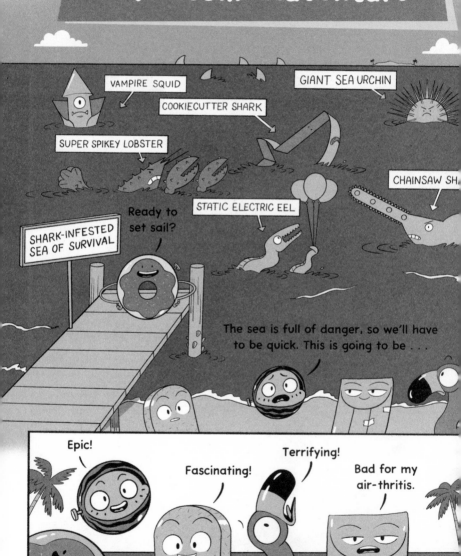

41

The oceanographer has arrived, ready to spot some wonderful watery wildlife.

HMS FLOATY BOAT

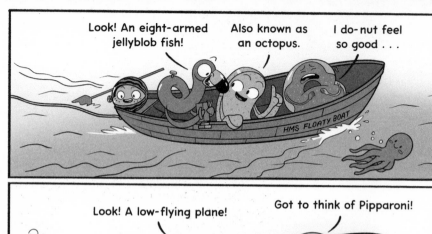

44

A lot of something elses.

I guess this is why it's called the
Shark-Infested Sea of Survival.
What are we going to do?

Angry dolphins!
Heeeeelp!!!!

MEGA COTTON-CANDY-FLAVORED FART

PFFFFFTTT!!

Malcolm, pass the
rotting whale carcass
air freshener!

So revolting.

Ewwww,
cotton candy!

48

49

We made it to dry land!

We shore did.

RECOVERY ICE BATH

But as exhausted as the inflata-friends were, if they [wa]nted to save Pipparoni, there was one thing to do . . .

Anyone feel like a nap?

I said there was one thing to do.

Oh, yes!

It's time to take on the desert.

# Chapter Six
# Don't Dessert Me Now

Well, here we are . . .

. . . THE DESERT ISLAND OF DOOM!

ALL I WANTED TO DO WAS FIND THE COOKIE OF CONTENTMENT

53

55

56

But a whole ten and a half seconds later, things had taken a turn.

We should never have left the Lost and Found pool! This trip was a worse idea than yogurt on pizza.

I'm too holey to be a hero.

Don't talk like that, inflata-mate. You gotta be-leaf in yourself!

We're SO close to the Cookie of Contentment. We just need to cross these dunes.

And watch out for that Spikius Maximus Cactus. One prickle and we'll be packing our bags for the recycling bin.

THE COOKIE OF CONTENTMEN

SPIKIUS MAXIMUS CACTUS

THE SPIKIEST CACTUS IN THE WORLD

THE GREAT SAND DUNES

59

65

# Chapter Seven
# A Bit of a Pickle

PRETZEL   PICKLE   ENCHILADA

THE LAST-EVER COOKIE
OF CONTENTMENT

69

... yeah ... I think it's donut ... um ... purple icing...okay, got it.

CLICK CLACK

GRUMPY RAINBOW

The Fickle Pickle says she loves donuts. She'll be out in a minute.

CLICK CLACK

GRUMPY RAINBOW

RECEPTION

COOKIE
TMENT

'mon, Donut-dude, you can't give up at the first hurdle.

We believe in you! You just have to go BIG.

• REC

THE DARING DONUT LOOKS LIKE HE MIGHT HAVE SOMETHING EXTRAORDINARY UP HIS INFLATABLE SLEEVE.

GRUMPY RAINBOW

RECEPTION

CLICK CLACK

Um . . . what if I said . . . please?

CLICK CLACK

74

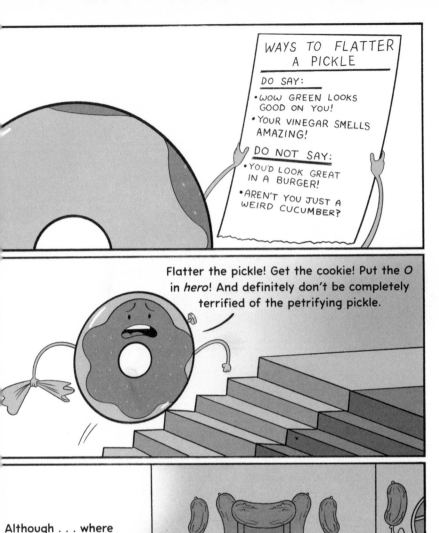

Flatter the pickle! Get the cookie! Put the O in *hero*! And definitely don't be completely terrified of the petrifying pickle.

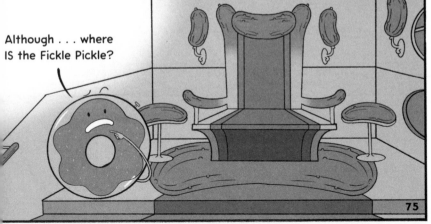

Although . . . where IS the Fickle Pickle?

Guys! She's not scary after all. She's just an itty-bitty pickle! Maybe even a cornichon! And no one has heard of them. It doesn't even rhyme with fickle!

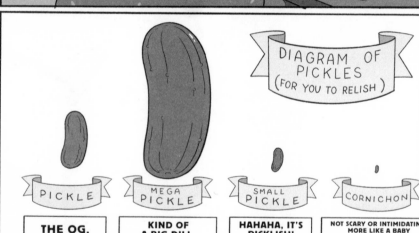

DIAGRAM OF PICKLES
(FOR YOU TO RELISH)

PICKLE

**THE OG.**

MEGA PICKLE

**KIND OF A BIG DILL.**

SMALL PICKLE

**HAHAHA, IT'S PICKLISH!**

CORNICHON

**NOT SCARY OR INTIMIDATING. MORE LIKE A BABY CUCUMBER, REALLY.**

What . . . Did . . . You . . . Say?!

77

# Chapter Eight

# It's Knot Me, It's You

That went well.

Do you think it was a yes?

Don't panic, Donut. There's always the other two guardians.

Maybe the Unimpressed Pretzel will help me?

79

Look, my friends and I have come all the way from Have a Great Spray Water Park. We've had air-mergencies, pop-mergencies, and butt-mergencies. And I haven't had a single slice of pizza the whole time!

Definitely not impressive. And it doesn't matter anyway . . .

That cookie isn't going anywhere unless all three guardians say yes. Ja. Sí. Oui. Hai.

That's "yes" in five languages. Which actually IS mildly impressive.

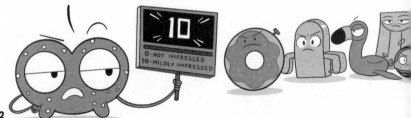

83

84

THE FICKLE PICKLE
LIVES HERE
(SOMETIMES)

SITE OF THE
LAST-EVER
COOKIE OF
CONTENTMENT

AHOOOO!!!

The Unimpressed Pretzel
is really unimpressed!

And the Energetic
Enchilada has just
started hover-boarding.

he Fickle Pickle
tes me (mostly).

You are all real heroes. And I'm an inflata-failure. What will I tell Pipparoni?

Don't cry, Donut! We need all the water we can get . . .

If it makes you feel better, I'm not going to win that Osc-air after all.

Why not, Flamingo? Donut's just having a moment. You can cut this part out.

No, it's because I was filming upside down! And I got cotton candy on the camera!! And I put Donut's camera on backward! All it filmed was his face!!!

·REC

87

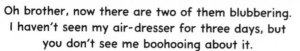

Oh brother, now there are two of them blubbering. I haven't seen my air-dresser for three days, but you don't see me boohooing about it.

Pause my prickles! This might not be that bad after all . . .

Donut, wait right there.

Good idea. If I melt, at least these weird desert bugs will have a wading pool.

Yay! I can practice my butterfly!

Hey, who's he calling weird?

91

**What? Is that really his name?!**

DONUT CAM ON
DONUT LOVES EVERY *BODY!*

DONUT CAM ON
DONUT CREATES A SWEET MEETING POINT!

STARRING

Donut Donutson as himself
(the hero)
Cactus
Flamingo
Watermelon
Lynn

WITH SPECIAL APPEARANCES BY

Skeleton
Gulper Sharks
Gummy Candies
Spikius Maximus Cactus
(aka Mikey)

CO-DIRECTOR   CO-DIRECTOR   STAR   CO-DIRECTOR   CO-DIRECTO

Thanks, guys. I can always count on my inflata-BIFFs.

**BEST INFLATABLE FRIENDS FOREVER**

I might not have gotten the cookie, but I'm not an inflata-failure. This Donut's going to save Pipparoni if it's the last thing I dough.

But the inflata-pals weren't the only ones watching Flamingo's mast-air-peace . . .

94

# Chapter Ten

# That's the Way the Cookie Crumbles

Bravo!

Wonderful!

That's hot!

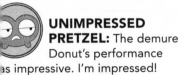

## Deflated Tomatoes

REVIEW

## DONUT OUR HERO

 **ENERGETIC ENCHILADA:** This film stopped me in my tracks! This guy is nacho average Donut. Taco 'bout a true hero!

RATING:  + 🔑

 **UNIMPRESSED PRETZEL:** The demure Donut's performance as impressive. I'm impressed! nd I'm knot kidding!

TING: 🥨🥨🥨🥨🥨 + 🔑

**FICKLE PICKLE:** It was incredible! But a little dull. A true masterpiece! With terrible acting. Donut is a hero for our times! And a little over-inflated. I love being called a cornichon!!

RATING: 🥒🥒🥒🥒🥒 + ???

95

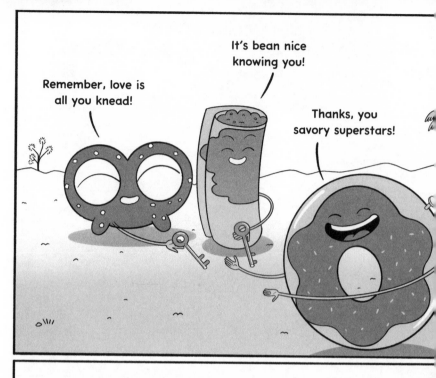

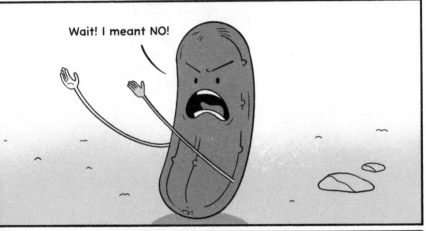

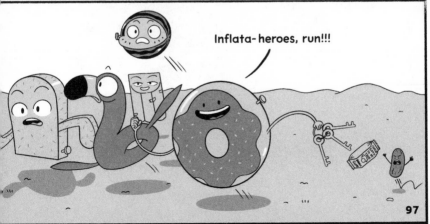

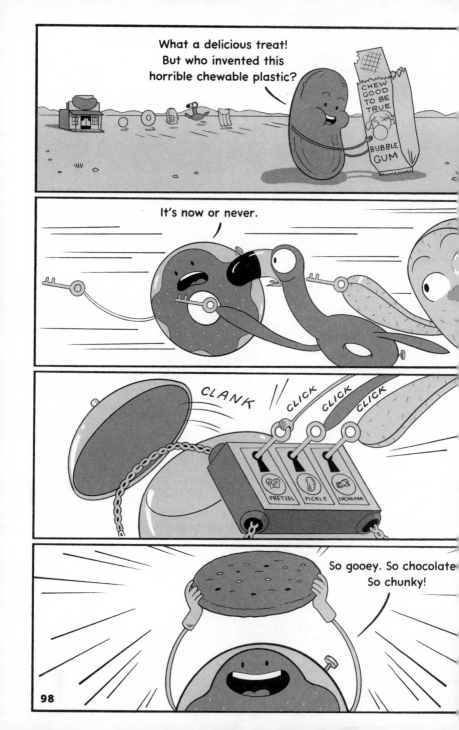

CHOMP

C'mon, Doughie, time to go!

104

OH, CRUMBS!

Don't you mean crumb.

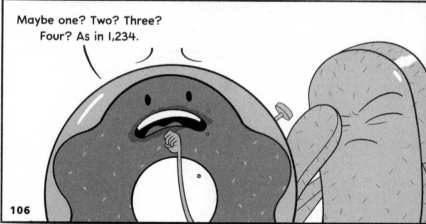

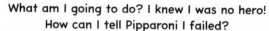

What am I going to do? I knew I was no hero! How can I tell Pipparoni I failed?

I was supposed to come back with a dessert so delicious it would save the pizza stand! Not a tiny crumb and some stomach cramps.

And a chocolate mustache.

It's time to tell Pipparoni the truth, Donut-dude. It's going to be tough. But so are you.

# Chapter Eleven

# Feast Your Pies on This

109

110

112

e launch of the
and improved
izza stand!

P'S SLIP
' SLICE!

MENU

PIP'S
SLIP-N-SLICE

OPEN

PIP'S

This . . . looks . . . ham-azing!

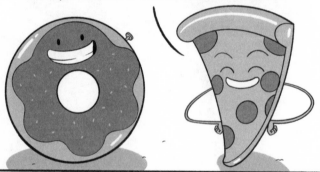

The stand wasn't closing down after all. It was getting even bigger! And thanks to you and your delicious trail of cookie crumbs . . .

. . . we've got the biggest crowd ever!

114

115

116

GULP!

Looks like it's time for a sea-quel!

Here we dough again . . .

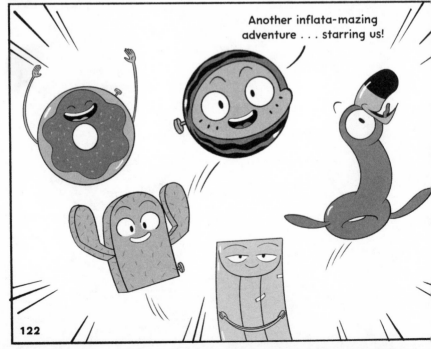

122

# THE INFLATABLES
## in SPLASH OF THE TITANS

Ready, set, BLOW! Have a Great Spray water park is hosting the Airlympic Games, and Watermelon is ready to juice her opponents—especially Pineapple, who's rotten to the core. But this year, the games are a team competition. Can Watermelon pump up her inflata-buddies to go for gold or will Pineapple's sneaky tricks deflate them all? It's do or dive time!

# THE INFLATABLES

## These bouncy besties are ready to make some waves!

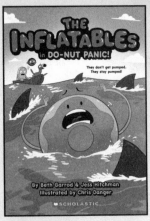